Anoth

E. Davis

Written by E. Davis
www.edavisllc.com

Published by Writers Block Publishing LLC

© Writers Block Publishing LLC 2017

All rights reserved

All characters in this book are fictitious, and any resemblance to real persons living or dead is coincidental.

Editing: by LitFixx and Writers Block Publishing LLC

Another Slice of Pie

ACKNOWLEDGMENT

I would like to thank my family and friends for allowing me to brainstorm and bounce ideas off them.

Second, I would like to acknowledge my muse. In 2006, I had a dream that an influential person will help me with my writing and whenever I am inspired to write, write.
It wasn't until 2008 that I was awakened to who that influential person would be. Never in my wildest dream did I ever think that he would be that person that would become my muse. Ever since then, whenever I happen to see him continually, that is purely coincidental; ideas and story ideas flow from me. I am not in his circle or among his friends, but just an admirer of his work. I find it humbling that the essence of him ignites my creativity. My work and words have nothing to do with his work, but the creative connection is beyond the comprehension of those who are not creative. However, at the risk of being long-winded and confusing, I would love to say thank you to Johnny Depp.

E. Davis

1

ANDREW SEES HER AT Ms. Ida's House of Soul, a local jazz lounge. Although this the first time he is seeing her, something is mesmerizing about her, and there was something about her that was familiar to him. Was it the way she wore the gardenias in her hair that paid tribute to the legendary Billie Holiday?

Where do I know her from? He asks himself.
Andrew couldn't stop staring because if he looks away or even an unconscious blink, he would miss her smile or the way she would curl her lips whenever she enunciates the words that she is singing. It is not just her familiar face that is intriguing to him. It was the words she sings,
That song, why is it so familiar? He asks himself.

"Excuse me?" Andrew said, summoning the waitress that is grabbing the dirty dishes from the tables beside him. She smiles at him,

"What is her name?"

"Lydia Rose," the waitress answers, then continues to clear the table.

Andrew looks back at Lydia, again questioning himself on why she looks so familiar.

"Excuse me," he summons the waitress again.

She smiles.

"Where is she from?" Andrew asks.

"I'm not sure," the waitress responds, smiling, then looks at Lydia. "She's good, huh?"

Andrew still can't put his finger on the mystery of her familiarity, Lydia Rose.

Why is she so familiar?

Another Slice of Pie

Andrew Gallagher is a prominent man in the city and a very wealthy, affluent African-American family member. The Gallagher Family is a shrewd but successful group of businessmen and women. Andrew's father, Nathaniel is an industrialist, businessman, entrepreneur, and his mother, Naomi, is a socialite. However, Andrew did not want to follow in the family's industrial footsteps. Instead, he became a successful novelist. Andrew is a handsome bachelor with light brown skin, hazel eyes, and a sweet smile. He has a gentleman-like demeanor that has made him quite desirable and adorable. There is a charming quality to him; he is generally a nice guy.

ANDREW ARRIVES HOME TO his penthouse in the Upper East Side apartment. Instead of being greeted by his current girlfriend, he is greeted by his maid, Mona Barrie.

"You still awake, Miss. Mona," Andrew said with a grin.

"Yes, came down here to fix me some tea. Would you like a cup?"

"Yes, that sounds good, thank you," he replies, taking his coat off and hanging it in the closet.

"How was your evening?" she asks.

"It was good," He answered.

Mona's skin is beautiful, with skin the color of copper. She is a petite woman, standing at an even five feet, and her gray hair is always pulled in a bun. She had been working for Andrew for fifteen years after the death of her husband. Mona mentioned that she lived alone. Andrew offered her a room for her to live in. Andrew didn't necessarily need a maid, but he enjoyed the company. Mona and Andrew's relationship is tender. She is more of a big sister who still looked after her little brother. She doesn't go to bed until

E. Davis

Andrew is home, and if she knows that he would not be home any particular night. At times they would stay up all night, drink tea, and talk about insignificant matters.

"Where's Lana?" Andrew asks.

"Right here," said a voice coming from upstairs.

Andrew looks upstairs and sees his current girlfriend, a young model that looks and smells like candy. Her skin is light brown like white sand. Her eyes are the color of emeralds, and she has long dark hair. Lana is a model that takes much pride in that she is an African-American model with such features. She stands at the top of the stairs looking sexy, wearing a black tank top and shorts that were so short that they look like panties. Andrew grins.

"Have you ever heard of the jazz singer Lydia Rose?" he asks Mona, still looking at Lana.

"No," Mona answers.

"Mona, I want some wine-red, please," Lana says, then walks away.

Andrew looks at Mona.

"I don't work for her," Mona said sternly.

Her brown eyes pierce into Andrew's eyes, Mona is not amused by the sweet candy that Andrew brought home every few months.

"Don't worry about the tea or wine, Miss Mona." He said with a chuckle, then rubs her shoulder.

"Good night, Mr. Gallagher," she says, then walks off.

Andrew sighs and then goes up the stairs to get a piece of candy.

IT'S WELL PAST MIDNIGHT Andrew is in his study trying to write. He starts to think about the spellbonding beauty that he saw earlier, Lydia Rose. He searches the internet looking for a search engine to look for information about her, but

Another Slice of Pie

there is nothing. She has such a familiar face as if he has seen her before, and the music is familiar as well. Andrew can't understand the sudden intrigue. Maybe she is a muse, something that is inspiring him. After some time, he gives up on his search and continues to write.

ANDREW AND LANA SIT in Miss. Ida's House of Soul. As far as Lana is concerned, this lounge is beneath her. She is a top runway model.

We don't dine in bars.

She cannot understand why someone like Andrew Gallagher would want to dine in a smoky bar. He is a Park Ave Prince; why not dine in something more prominent or clean.

"I like the music, I like the food, I like the place, Lana," Andrew would tell her.

The audience waits for Miss. Ida to take the stage to introduce the performer of the evening.

"Ladies and gentlemen, Miss. Lydia Rose," Miss Ida says.

Applause goes forth from the audience, and Lydia Rose takes the stage. She looks beautiful in a coral-colored A-line baby-doll dress that comes to her knees. Like Billie, she has the gardenia in her hair. Lydia looks like an exotic beauty; again, where does he know her from? There is something about her dark eyes and her smile.

"ANDREW!" Lana yells.

He looks at her. She looks irritated.

"I asked you a question!"

"What?" he asked.

"Never mind," she replies, irritated.

"Lana, what, I'm sorry,"

"I'm ready to leave," Lana says, gathering her purse and shawl.

Quickly Lana stands and begins to leave.

"Leave? Lana, we just got here!" He says, standing to prepare to follow her.

"This song is an oldie but goodie," Lydia says.

The music begins to play a recognizable song catching Andrew's attention. Then Lydia starts to sing, and then suddenly, that strange familiarity becomes quite clear.

"Robin," he mouths the name.

This woman on stage cannot be Robin, she is too young, but the resemblance is uncanny because she looks just like Robin. Quickly Andrew looks back, wanting to go after Lana, but he cannot move. The image of Robin is holding him in place. The music, the familiarity of the songs, those songs that Lydia Rose sings is Robin's lyrics. That oldie but goodie that Lydia is singing was Robin's favorite song; Andrew knows this by the way Lydia is singing the song.

"Excuse me," said a waiter. "If you can, please sit down; they can't see in the back."

Andrew quickly sits down and continues to stare at the image of an old and familiar friend.

ANDREW WAITS TO THE end of Lydia's performance. He needs to talk to her. He approaches the bartender.

"Can I speak with Lydia Rose?" he asks.

The bartender shakes his head.

"Sorry, she leaves immediately after her session."

Andrew sighs,

"Will she be in tomorrow?" Andrew asks.

The bartender nods his head. Andrew thanks the bartender for the little information, and then he races home. The anxiety of the possibility of who Lydia Rose is or who she might be weighs heavily on Andrew's heart. He storms into the house, startling Mona.

Another Slice of Pie

"Mr. Gallagher," Mona says, startled by his frantic demeanor.

"Get me something to drink, strong!" he exclaims, then raced into his study.

He opens the closet and pulls out a photo box. Mona enters in with his brandy. Andrew opens the box and dumps the photos on the floor. He sits down on the floor and searches frantically through them.

"Mr. Gallagher," Mona says. "What's the matter?"

Andrew doesn't reply. He grabs a photo of a beautiful black woman. She has dark eyes and a bright smile and rose in her hair and again the uncanny resemblance because the woman looks like Lydia.

"AHHHH!" he cries out. "ROBIN!"

Mona stands nervously, not knowing what she should do. Andrew is breathing hard. Her name: Lydia Rose; that is his name.

"Robin," he groans.

"Mr. Gallagher," Mona says in a soft tone.

She walks to him and sits down beside him on the floor.

"What is the matter?"

Andrew looks at Mona. She sees pain in his eyes.

"The singer," he said softly.

Tears fall from his eyes. Mona nods but doesn't know what he is referring to.

"She's my baby," Andrew says.

Mona's eyes question asking, trying to understand who and what he is talking about. Andrew shows her the picture that is in his hand. Mona looks at the photo then she looks at him. She shrugs her shoulders in bewilderment.

E. Davis

"We were married, but she left me," Andrew said in a soft tone. "I wanted her to stay, but she wouldn't. She must have been pregnant; I didn't know it, and tonight, that singer. She's my child."

Mona is shocked by what Andrew is telling her. Then she begins to remember, few years before she started working for him. Everyone in the city was shocked by Andrew's impromptu marriage to a local girl he happened to have gone to college with. However, with their low-key lifestyle and minimal social sightings, Andrew Gallagher's marriage became no big deal. Most people predicted that she would be gone in a few years, and she was; two years later.

"How old is the child?" Mona asked.

"She has to be about twenty-two," he answers. "I have to talk to Robin."

Andrew quickly stands and races to the door.

"Mr. Gallagher," Mona calls out quickly, jumping up to grab Andrew.

"I have to talk to Robin-,"

"It's well past midnight," she points to the digital clock on his desk.

"But-,"

"Do you know where she is?" Mona asks.

Andrew thinks. He has no idea where Robin is, and Lydia is gone. He has to wait until the next day. He sighs.

"Sit down," Mona says, leading him to the sofa.

She hands him his drink and sits down beside him.

"Are you sure that the girl is your daughter?"

"Yes," he answers as he quickly drinks the bandy.

He hands Mona the glass. Mona raises the glass indicating if he wants another. He shakes his head. Mona looks at him with questions in her eyes.

Another Slice of Pie

"She looks like her mother as if she spit her out. The music that she sang said Robin all over it, and her name, Lydia Rose, I always said that if I had a daughter, her name would be Lydia, Lydia Rose Gallagher."

"Okay, so then why wouldn't she tell you about the baby? How did you not know that she was pregnant?"

"Robin was-," he takes a deep breath, then he slowly exhales. "I want to be alone."

Mona grins,

"Okay," she says; then she stands. "If you need anything,"

Andrew nods then watches Mona leave. He takes in another deep breath and thinks about Robin.

Robin Booker, his ex-wife, from the start, their marriage was a hoax, a temporary convenience to buy time. However, within the course of this marriage, they fell in love with each other. Andrew wanted to make the marriage real, but Robin didn't want a commitment. And when the time came to move on, she left, leaving Andrew heartbroken. He has never been the same emotionally. Although he dated many women, he never remarried. Instead, he dated a variety of women for temporary comfort. Andrew wondered why she left him. Was it because of Lydia? He would have done the right thing. He would have taken care of the baby without hesitation and without question. Robin avoided emotional contact and the concept of commitment. But Andrew could look into Robin's eyes and see that she loved him, and the few times they made love; he could tell that she loved him. But Robin was adamant about her decision. She enjoyed their friendship, but she did not want a relationship.

Andrew is confident that Lydia Rose is his child, his daughter. Her look, her style, and the music all spoke of Robin.

E. Davis

Still thinking about Lydia Rose, Andrew can see she's a Gallagher.

Is Lydia from here? He asks himself. Is she local? If so, why haven't I seen her? Where is Robin?

Andrew looks out of the window; the moon shines directly in front of the window. He thinks about Lana; maybe he should go upstairs to see what her problem was.

Why did she run out of the club so quickly? He asks himself.

Andrew can't bring himself to move. His mind is running, and his thoughts are occupied; he decides that he doesn't want any candy, but as he turns away from the window, candy is at the door.

Lana enters the study wearing a short black lacy nightgown. Andrew looks at her, but he shows no emotion. Lana sits down beside him.

"Why did you leave?" he coolly.

"Why did you stay?" she asks.

Then she looks at the pictures on the floor.

"What's going on?" she asks.

Looking at her, Andrew shakes his head. Lana shrugs her shoulders, not caring to press the issue.

"You coming to bed," she asks.

"In a minute," he answers.

Just as he watched her come into the study, Andrew watches her leave. Still, he doesn't move from the couch.

IN SPITE OF ALL THAT he is feeling, he managed to doze off only to sleep for a few hours. Mona awakens him. She has breakfast and coffee for him.

Another Slice of Pie

"You okay?" she asks.

"I guess," he answers.

"Are you going to that lounge?" Mona asks.

Andrew nods his head.

"I have a few meetings today, but I will be there."

Mona walks to the photos that are still on the floor. She kneels and picks up the pictures and puts them in the box. She looks at a picture of Andrew and Robin sitting together. In the photo, they are smiling.

"You two seemed happy," Mona comments.

Andrew sips his coffee.

2

The summer was hot, the beach was crowded, but Andrew did not mind the heat. The smell of the ocean water almost intoxicated him, and the loud, bright colors that the tourist wore nearly blinded him. Andrew didn't like being out in the sun, but he enjoyed the scenery of a bright sunny day. So he stayed inside at the cabana sipping on a Bahama Mama. Andrew scanned the scenery. There was a type of tranquility here. A two-week vacation on an island, watching romantic refuges cook a pig over a fire, and he observed the tourists wander on the beach. Here, Andrew was able to escape the pressures of school, work, and his controlling family, the notorious Gallaghers.

Andrew did not know how to tell his father that he did not want to follow in the family business. Andrew wanted his way. He wanted to be a writer, to make his living with his pen. It was important to him to establish his own identity, not to be accepted in society because he is a Gallagher. Andrew didn't know how he was going to tell his father this, the Great Nathaniel Gallagher. Nathaniel was a man that most small businessmen owners feared. He was a tyrant. When he spoke, people listened, and the word no did not come easily unless it came out of his mouth. However, Andrew had two weeks to think about how he was going to tell his father no.

As Andrew sipped on his drink, he spotted a familiar beauty approaching the bar, Robin Booker. He and Robin attended the same college, and they had a few classes together.

"Robin," he called out.

Another Slice of Pie

Robin looked over; her moon-shaped eyes caught him off guard.

Was she this pretty in class? He thought.

She approached him with a polite grin on her face.

"Hi," he said, smiling.

She looked at him, wondering where she knew him from. She then grinned when she remembered.

"Adam Goodson," she guessed.

"Andrew Gallagher," he politely corrected.

"Right, sorry," Robin said, almost embarrassed.

"What can I get you," the bartender asked.

Robin looked at Andrew's drink,

"Whatever he's drinking," she answered. "So, how you been?"

"Good," he answered. "You,"

"Good. Enjoying a little R & R," she said smiling.

"Me too," he responded.

They sat quietly for a moment while the bartender made Robin's drink.

"So, how long you been here?" Andrew asked.

"I've been here since this morning," she told him. "I'm here for two weeks. What about you?"

"The same," he said. "Came in today, leave in about two weeks. Soaking up some sun,"

"The sun is not in here," she said with a chuckle.

The bartender handed her the drink.

"No, but the view is nice," Andrew said as she scanned the crowd. "Are you here with anyone?"

"No what about you?"

"Solo," Andrew said.

Robin attempted to hand the bartender money,

"I got it," Andrew said with a grin.

"Um, thanks," Robin said, somewhat surprised. "Well, enjoy the rest of your vacation, hope to see you around."

"You too,"

Robin walked away.

Call it fate or coincidence or just two lonely people in need of company. Throughout the week, Robin and Andrew managed to spend their vacation together. They found themselves looking for one another while enjoying the fresh fruit for breakfast in the morning. They found it easy to talk to each other. Robin and Andrew attended the tourist activities together, such as snorkeling, dancing on the sand during the pig roasting, and relaxing on the beach. Andrew and Robin both lived in New York, Andrew in Manhattan, and Robin in Brooklyn. Andrew learned that Robin, too, was a writer, a songwriter. Robin knew of the Gallagher family, but she couldn't understand why Andrew couldn't tell his father that he wanted to write.

"Just tell him what you want to do," Robin said to Andrew one night.

Andrew had been telling her about some of his concerns with telling his family about wanting to write.

"It's not that easy, plus no one will take me seriously if I am not in business with my father."

"People will take you seriously. You're Andrew Gallagher. You could own the world if you wanted to."

Andrew smiled at her. She was pretty. Robin wore a cream-colored sundress with white gardenias in her hair. The full moon and the navy blue-colored sky as her background made her look like a beautiful moon goddess. Together they walked along the beach, both of them holding their sandals in their hands.

"So why haven't I heard any of your songs on the radio." Andrew inquired.

Another Slice of Pie

"I had some distractions," Robin said coolly. "I always wanted my recording studio."

"So what stopping you now?"

"I'm not a Gallagher," Robin joked.

Andrew chuckled.

"No, seriously, I am currently working at a dead-end job, saving money, hoping that one day some nightclub diva makes it big singing one of my songs. I would love to have a baby grand piano, where I can sit and write music all day."

"What brought you to the islands alone?" Andrew asked.

"Trying to clear my head from those distractions," Andrew sighed. "Other than my dad, uh, well, there is this girl, Courtney. I grew up with her, her family, and my family wants us to get married, but I don't want to marry her,"

"Then don't," Robin said with a chuckle.

"It's not that easy, Robin. In my family, you do as you're told or find your way. In my family's eyes, marrying Courtney is a good business opportunity."

"Oh my goodness!" Robin exclaimed. "You're family acts like some middle eastern folk. Arranged marriages? What happened to the good old days when people married for love? Oh, wait a minute, those weren't the good old days; that's today!"

"I can't just go to my dad and say, 'No, I want to do things my way,' or 'No, I'm not going to marry Courtney,' but-,"

"You're spoiled," Robin stated. "You're a spoiled little boy that is afraid of his daddy."

They stopped walking. Andrew stood still shocked by Robin's commit. She continued.

E. Davis

"So what? Your dad will get mad because you're not working for the family. As far as that Courtney girl, forget that girl. You're a grown man. So what you're not working for your family may get you cut off from the family fortune. Learn to make it on your own, and your self-worth will be greater than the Gallagher Empire."

Andrew sighed,

"You're right," he said. "I will, but I just need time, though."

"So this is what this vacation is doing? Buying you time." Robin interrogated.

Andrew nodded his head,

"To come up with a plan," he said.

"If I come up with a plan, then yeah, I can say, 'Dad, this is what I want to do, and this is how long,'-,"

"I cannot believe you need a drafted proposal for your dad to let you live your life."

There was a slight wind, a gentle breeze causing Robin to shiver a little. Andrew took off his jacket and placed it on Robin's shoulders. She looked up at him and thanked him with a grin.

"Thanks," she said, smiling.

Andrew nodded his head. There was a gentle nature about him, a soft and quiet manner. The Gallagher family was a notorious family. They were not scandalous, but their business tactics and strategies were crafty, sometimes cunning. If one would contend with them, they needed to be highly intelligent, able to stand with confidence in the midst of them. Showing no sign of weakness and being able to look each one in the eyes.

Robin chuckled.

Another Slice of Pie

"I hear about your dad, that he was a beast in the boardroom. Just the mention of his name gets him the best table in the restaurants; gets him the best seats in the theater. But never did I think that the mention of his name has you shaking in your shorts."

"My father is a mighty man, maybe because, as a black man, he had to prove himself. Prove that you are worth standing with them. I'm not refereeing to the powerful black man aspect of it; you know what I mean?"

Robin nodded her head,

Andrew continued.

"He came from nothing, I mean dirt poor, and he had people telling him that he was dumb. But there was a determination in his soul; he wouldn't be defeated, he may have been born poor, but he refused to die poor. Am I saying his tactics are right? No. But him being ignorant, being stupid, being lazy is not an option. If he thinks you come up short because you are lazy, then you're considered to be disgraced."

Robin listened attentively as they continued their walk on the beach. Once they arrived back at their hotel, they bid each other good night and said that they would see each other for breakfast in the morning.

It was during dinner the next day that Andrew had the strangest idea. It was the perfect plan to deal with Nathaniel Gallagher and to discourage any idea that the Gallagher family had for him and Courtney.

"Excuse me," Robin asked, almost offended at his suggestion.

"Marriage," Andrew said holding his breath. "We can get married. It can buy me time to take care of business. It can be a business deal."

"A business deal," Robin asked. "If this is a business deal, then marry that girl."

"No," Andrew said. "If I marry Courtney, both our families will expect children."

"And they won't want us to conceive a child?"

"No, my parents wouldn't approve of our marriage-,"

"Thanks," she said sarcastically.

"No, you're not from the same side; they wouldn't want us to be married, let alone have a child. Us; will be strictly business, we won't consummate, just be legally married. Give me two years, and we can get a divorce. By then, Courtney's family will have her tied to someone else, and I will have what I want."

"What is that?" Robin asked.

"My identity," Andrew answered.

Robin chuckled.

"You're going to find yourself in two years; no, thank you. Besides, I don't even know you; you can be some monster!"

"Have you known of my family or me to be monsters?"

"From what you have told me about them this past week-,"

"Okay, okay," Andrew said, putting his hands up in a surrender. "Controlling yes; monsters no."

"No, thank you?" Robin said, shaking her head.

"I'll pay you,"

"No," she said. "What is the matter with you?!"

"Just think, Robin, you can use the money for that studio," Andrew said suggestively.

Robin sat back in her seat and took in a deep breath. Andrew saw that he had reached her.

Another Slice of Pie

"Robin, it is just business, nothing more. Whatever you need for your studio, I will pay. You can quit that customer service job. Spend the day playing on your baby grand writing and playing your music. Robin, you and I are both writers; we need to write. Wouldn't it be nice just to write all day?"

Her eyes never left Andrew's eyes. For the first time since she ran into him on this vacation, she saw the determination in his eyes. In college, he was Andrew Gallagher, son of Nathaniel Gallagher. The girls seemed fixated on him, but that was only because of his name. Nothing was appealing about him, nothing incredibly intriguing. His actions were typical for a spoiled rich kid; everything was given to him. However, throughout this week, Robin saw an easy-going guy that loves to dream, but she also saw a man that would be considered spineless. Despite this, Andrew's plan seemed crazy, ridiculous, and outlandish, but the determination she saw in his eyes was powerful. He was willing to pay. At that very moment, Robin thought of the debt that she could pay off. She can have that music studio, her music studio, and that baby grand. She finally broke from Andrew's stare.

"I just need two years," he said in a soft tone.

"Living arrangements?" she asked.

Andrew grinned.

"I can rent a place, a three-bedroom apartment; we have our room. My family is socialites; we make a few social sightings just to give the appearance of a happy couple, and then after two years, we divorce, citing irreconcilable differences."

Robin shook her head. "

No, I'll look like the bad guy, and my dreams will fade,"

E. Davis

"I promise," Andrew said, placing his right hand on his heart. "I will not let you be bad-mouthed."

"You honestly think people will buy that you and I are a happy couple."

"We leave in seven days. That gives us a week to get to know each other; we can prove our love," he said with a smirk.

Robin slowly inhaled, then exhaled, and then she nodded.

They found a justice of the peace, and they got married.

That evening instead of physically consummating their marriage, they got straight down to business, spending the night getting to know each other. Robin was born in August, and Andrew was a New Year baby. His favorite color was green, and her favorite color was blue, royal blue the best. When it came down to family matters, Robin had two brothers, Xavier and James; she is the youngest. In the days following, Andrew and Robin spent every hour together to have the appearance of newlyweds in love. They practiced holding each other hands. It seemed uncomfortable at first, but after a while, holding each other hands felt, good almost natural. Sometimes Andrew and Robin would find themselves enjoying the comfort of looking into each other's eyes, and there was a type of serenity in their being with each other.

Once they arrived back in New York, Andrew took Robin to her apartment and told her that he would come back for her in a few hours to go to his family's for dinner.

✦

They stood speechless, their eyes wide, not blinking as they stared at the brown beauty. She was beautiful, yes.

Another Slice of Pie

She wore a lavender button-up silk blouse with dark trousers and a pearls string necklace from Andrew lay elegantly upon her neck. Her dark hair was pinned up in a bun, but what was most impressive was the eight-karat diamond ring on her finger. Andrew took a deep breath.

"This is Robin Booker, ah, Gallagher, my wife." He said nervously.

There was an eternal ten to fifteen-second pause. Andrew swallowed a gulp.

"Robin, meet my father, Nathaniel Gallagher, my mother, Naomi, my brother Ethan and my sister Stephanie."

"Your wife?" Naomi asked, surprised.

"Yes," Andrew answered "We got married while I was away,"

"Did you go away to get married?" Naomi asked.

"No, I met Robin back in school. I happened to have run into her while on the island. One thing led to another-,"

"One thing led to another?" Nathaniel asked.

"Ah," Naomi said nervously, "Robin, It is nice to meet you."

Naomi extended her hand to Robin to shake.

"The pleasure is mine, Mrs. Gallagher," Robin said, shaking Naomi's hand.

Then she shook the hands of Ethan and Stephanie. Robin looked at Nathaniel; he reluctantly shook her hand.

"Andrew, a word," Nathaniel said sternly.

Robin and Andrew quickly glanced at each other then she watched Andrew walked away with his father.

"Robin, please sit down and make yourself at home."

Robin, Naomi, Ethan, and Stephanie sat down. The silence was awkward. The maid sat a tray of coffee on the table.

"Would you like some coffee?" Naomi asked.

"No, thank you," Robin said politely.

Naomi grinned,

"So, ah, you went to school with Andrew?"

"Yes, we had a statistic class together,"

"What did you study?"

"I majored in English," Robin answered.

Naomi seemed impressed.

"What do you do?"

Robin grinned,

"I am a customer service representative for an insurance company."

The impressed look on Naomi's face quickly went away. She glanced at her two children, who were trying hard not to stare at their mother. Meanwhile, in the den a few rooms down, Nathaniel stood still, looking at his son. Andrew, the middle child, the most lackadaisical in his ways, goes to some island and brings home a wife. Not a tacky souvenir but a no-name girl whom he met in college almost four years ago.

"What is going on?" Nathaniel asked.

"Nothing," Andrew said with a grin, "I fell in love,"

"Just like that,"

"Yep,"

"What about Courtney?"

"Courtney was your plan, not mine," Andrew commented.

Nathaniel wanted to strangle his son. "You have a better plan with this girl?"

"Dad, Robin, is a good girl," Andrew said. "I love her, that's it. I didn't want to marry Courtney, never did."

"So, tell me, what is that you love so much about this Robin?"

Andrew had to think quickly. What about Robin made him love her, or liked, or something to appease his father? If

Another Slice of Pie

he says her beauty, then he is looked upon as a shallow boy, and he married her for the sex.

"Robin is challenging. She makes you think. She is also modest. She is reserved and quiet. She doesn't talk just to be heard, but she speaks when she has something to say."
Nathaniel grinned,

"Lovely qualities for a young woman to have, especially if she is trying to impress the son of a multi-millionaire."

"Dad, it's not like that,"

"I am having a prenup drafted immediately."

"One has already been arranged," Andrew said quickly.

"Oh," Nathaniel said, surprised. "What are the terms?"

"I don't think that none of your business,"

Insulted, Nathaniel tried not to let his anger come into full throttle. He took in a deep breath.

"When it comes to my money, it is my business,"

You're not the only shrewd businessman on the block. I managed to take my trust fund and make wise investments."

As simple-minded as Andrew could be, Nathaniel was aware that Andrew had stock in a few major businesses.

"Robin is not the only thing that I wanted to tell you," Andrew said. "I am going to focus on my writing."

"You're writing?" Nathaniel asked.

"Yes, I am going to be a writer," Andrew said. "Effective today, I am turning in my resignation."

Shocked and stunned Nathaniel stood still. Andrew put his hands in his pockets and walked out of the den. Nathaniel quickly followed.

"Robin," Andrew said.

E. Davis

Immediately Robin stood up and walked towards Andrew. Naomi also stood up.

"He just quit!" Nathaniel said to Naomi.

"Quit?" Naomi said, shocked. "Andrew,"

"He's going to be a writer," Nathaniel said mockingly.

"Mom, we have to go," Andrew said, taking hold of his mother's hands.

"Go," she asked. "Andrew, stay, let's talk about this,"

"Mom, we can't stay," Andrew said.

"But-," she tried to interject.

Andrew looked back and saw his father looking at his mother. Andre then looked at his mother.

"Mom, we'll call you later," Andrew said.

He hugged and kissed his mother.

Andrew grabbed Robin's hand, and they escaped. Once they got into the car, Andrew raced off.

"Where are we going?" Robin asked.

"Your place?" he said.

"My place, why my place," Robin asked surprisingly.

"Because I need a change of scenery,"

Robin sighed,

What have I gotten myself into? She asked herself.

Once they arrived at Robin's apartment, she watches as he began to paces the floor.

Robin walked to the refrigerator to grab a beer. She handed it to Andrew. He took the drink.

"Did you think they would be thrilled?" Robin asked sarcastically.

"No, but-,"

Andrew began to calm down. He walked across Robin's apartment, a brownstone. She had modest yet chic brown and green furniture. There was a keyboard in the back of the living room. He saw sheet music on the floor.

Another Slice of Pie

"So when do we tell your family?" Andrew asked.

"I don't have to answer to my family as you do. I am an adult." She stated.

She looked at Andrew; he was daydreaming the window,

"Andrew," he didn't hear her call his name.

3

"ANDREW," ANDREW IS STARTLED. His good friend and publisher Wayne Ruple calls out his name. Andrew looks at him.

"Where were you?"

"I gotta go," Andrew said, quickly standing up.

"Go, go where?" Wayne asked. "Andy, your book is due; we need to go over,"

"Wayne, I will call you later, I promise."

Andrew quickly leaves Wayne puzzled and somewhat irritated. He drives out of the parking lot, and he drives to Ida's House of Soul.

He enters and approaches the bartender, who is drying the glasses.

"Excuse me," Andrew begin; the bartender looked up. "Is Lydia Rose here?"

"No, Ms. Lydia won't be here until five."

Andrew looks at his watch. It read two-thirty. He hesitates to move.

"Um, okay, thank you,"

The bartender grins.

"She's bad, ain't she?" the bartender says, shaking his head. "Mmm, Ms. Lydia is something else. Can I ask who is looking for her?"

"Ah, yes, Andrew Gallagher," Andrew answers

Andrew thanks the bartender then leaves.

ANDREW DRIVES HOMES. HE sits in his den looking out of the window. He takes a picture of Robin and him out of his pocket and looks at it. In this picture, he and Robin had been married for a month. Andrew had acquired them a penthouse

Another Slice of Pie

apartment for them. It had two floors and four bedrooms. Robin had sub-rented her apartment until her lease ran out. The one clause in the marriage was not to date anyone or have any personal relations during the marriage. This marriage was supposed to look as real as possible.

    As promised, Andrew brought Robin a beautiful ebony-colored baby grand piano. Immediately, Robin began to play. So far living together did not seem difficult. They had respect for each other's personal space while at the same time enjoying each other's company. They would have breakfast or dinner together without realizing they were dining together. They would sit and watch television together without taking notice that they were enjoying each other's company. Whenever either of them was working-writing, and they were not ready to eat dinner, lunch, or breakfast, one would prepare a plate and set it aside to come to it later. It was the typical activities of a married couple. Other than the absence of physical intimacy, they seemed to be a perfect couple.

    One particular evening, Andrew was out running some errand. When he came home, he found Robin playing the piano. He loved to hear her play. He also loved to watch her as she tickled the keys.

    "Who taught you how to play?" Andrew asked.

    "My grandmother, her name was Rosie Lee, she was cool."

    "Rose?" Andrew asked.

    Robin nodded.

    "I like the name Rose," Andrew said. "I always said that if I had a daughter, her name would be Lydia Rose."

    Robin grinned and focused back on the music. She started to play the song, *Killing Me Softly*,

E. Davis

"This is my favorite song," she said.

"Why?"

Robin thought about her answer. She closed her eyes and began to feel the music. She opened her eyes and looked at Andrew.

"I don't know," she answered. "The melody is pretty, the lyrics are-," Robin sighed with contentment, "I just love this song,"

Andrew continued to listen to her play. She was an amazing pianist. He listened to her play the classics from Bach to Beethoven. She played more contemporary R&B classics from artists like Stevie Wonder and Donnie Hathaway. Later that evening, they sat by the fire, ate pizza, and drank wine.

"What is your favorite book," Robin asked.

Andrew thought for a moment,

"I cannot say that I have a favorite book, but *To Kill a Mocking Bird*, was a good book. What about you? What's your favorite book?"

"*The Catcher in the Rye*," Robin answered.

Andrew looked at her for a moment, shocked by her answer. He laughed quietly.

"What?" Robin asked, trying to read the message with his chuckle.

She smiled.

"That is an unusual favorite for a girl," Andrew said.

"Excuse me," she said, laughing.

"I mean, women like books like *Little Women*, *Pride and Prejudice*, *Waiting to Exhale*-,"

"So *The Catcher in the Rye* is a boys' book?

"No," Andrew said, smiling.

Another Slice of Pie

He was going to speak, but he hesitated then started laughing.

"*To Kill a Mocking Bird* is a little girl's point of view on some issues," Robin said, sipping her wine.

Andrew just grinned and then sipped his wine.

"You ever read *The Catcher in the Rye?*" Robin asked.

Andrew nodded his head,

"Yeah, I've read it, back in high school; required reading." he began, "A lot of serial killers have a copy of the book, you know."

Robin laughed. She looked at Andrew with a mischievous grin. Andrew smiled.

"Do you have a copy of that book?" Andrew asked.

Robin sipped her wine and continued to look at him. Playfully she glared at him. He found Robin amusing the way she was trying to come across be devious. She started laughing.

"Tell me why you like it so much?"

Robin thought for a moment,

"The hope of redemption,"

It was quiet for a moment.

"What do you hope for?" Andrew asked.

Robin looked at Andrew there were questions in his eyes. He desired to know her intimate secrets.

What makes you tick, Robin Booker?

At times, she seemed so guarded and stand-offish. Whenever he thinks he saw a sparkle of light in her eyes, whenever he thinks that she may share something with a friend, she pulls back. She shuts down, and that sparkle disappears, and she becomes just Robin; a casual acquaintance. Someone to make small talk with.

Evasively, she looked away. He saw that she withdrew herself from this subject.

E. Davis

"How's your writing?" she asked, not looking at him.

"It's coming," he said, allowing the subject to be changed.

The mood in the air shifted. Both seemed to be uncomfortable; did he get too close? Did he ask something too personal?

"My writing is coming along well," Andrew answered.

She noticed the pizza box. There was nothing but crust left inside. She looked at Andrew.

"Well, I am going to turn in," she said.

"Okay,"

Together they both stood up. Andrew grabbed the pizza box to throw away. Robin went to bed.

This abrupt end of an enjoyable evening seemed strange to Andrew. The next morning Andrew was wakened to Robin playing, *Killing Me Softly.*

✦

ANDREW RETURNED TO THE lounge. He hears laughing and music playing. The bartender recognizes Andrew. He nods his head towards Andrew, acknowledging him. Andrew grins.

"Lydia!" the bartender calls out, "Lydia,"

Lydia finally emerges from the back. Andrew's heart races rapidly in his chest. There is a lump in his throat, and his mouth was dry.

"Someone's here to see you, babe,"

Lydia looks to Andrew; she smiles at him. By the way, she is wearing her long hair. She looks so much like Robin. She wears a simple red T-shirt and a pair of jeans. She extends her hand to Andrew.

"Hi, I'm Lydia," she said, smiling.

Another Slice of Pie

"Andrew Gallagher," Andrew shakes her hand.

"Andrew Gallagher, the writer?" she asks.

"Yes,"

"I enjoy your work," she said, smiling.

"Ah, thank you," Andrew said, caught off guard. "Ah, if it is all right, I have some business that I would like to discuss,"

"Oh?" Lydia said, raising her eyebrow, again looking like Robin. "What kind of business?"

Andrew slowly inhales, then he slowly exhales. Before he can answer, a tall, dark-skinned man approached.

"Excuse me, I'm Derrick Hughes, Ms. Rose's manager," he says, standing behind Lydia placing his hand on her shoulder.

"Nice to meet you, Mr. Hughes, but my business is with Ms. Rose," Andrew said smiling.

Lydia grins. She politely glances at Derrick and then focuses on Andrew.

"Mr. Gallagher, can I talk with you tonight, at ten?"

"Yes," Andrew replied. "Can we meet at Café Madden?"

"Okay," Lydia said. "See you then."

4

ANDREW WAITS FOR LYDIA at Café Madden, a local diner run by a friendly Notre Dame fan named Mike Madden, his wife, Verna, and their daughter Missy. Andrew sees Lydia walking into the diner. He stands to greet her.

"Ms. Rose, thank you for meeting me," he says

"Lydia," she told him, smiling.

"Lydia," Andrew said.

Together they sit down. Missy approaches them.

"Hi, Andrew," Missy says, smiling.

"Hi, Missy. Ah, can I have a coffee, black, and-," he looked directly at Lydia, "You get whatever you want."

Lydia grins.

"Tea with an orange wedge," she says.

"Is Ms. Verna's apple pie available?" Andrew asks.

"Yep," Missy answers with a chuckle.

"Ms. Verna's pie is to die for."

Andrew says to Lydia,

"Is that right?" Lydia says, smiling.

Andrew nods his head.

"I will have to try a slice," Lydia says, smiling.

"Okay, black coffee, tea with an orange wedge, and two slices of mom's pie; got it," Missy said, then walked away.

Andrew takes in a deep breath. Lydia grins.

"Do you come here a lot," she asks.

"At least once or twice a week to write,"

"I read all of your books," Lydia grins. "I really enjoy your books,"

"Thank you," he said modestly. "Your performance tonight was amazing!"

"Thank you, Mr. Gallagher,"

Another Slice of Pie

"Andrew," he said.

Lydia nods her head.

"Ah, the reason why I asked to meet with you tonight-,"

Andrew is interrupted by Missy bringing out their food.

"Thanks, Missy,"

"Sure, need anything, just yell," she said with a grin.

As Missy walks away, Andrew takes a bite of the apple pie; then, he closes his eyes with satisfaction.

"Mmm, Ms. Verna, Ms. Verna," he said, licking his lips.

Lydia then takes a bit, and she too went:

"Mmm,"

"Told you," Andrew said, smiling. "I've been begging Ms. Verna for the recipe, but she won't budge, but I will get it."

"This pie is really good," Lydia said, taking another bite of the pie. "My mom used to make a good apple pie, but this pie is really good."

"Your mom," Andrew said.

Lydia nods. He takes in another deep breath then sips his coffee.

"Um, the reason why I asked to meet with you is, well, I ah, I don't know where to start. Your mother, her name is Robin Booker, right?"

"Yes," Lydia answered. "Did you know my mom?"

Andrew looks away,

"May I ask how old you are?"

"I'm twenty-two," she answers.

Still not looking at her, he nodded his head. "When's your birthday?"

"March,"

E. Davis

It is quiet for a moment, Andrew's heartbreaks. He doesn't know what to say or what to do. He has to look at her. He has to face her. Lydia sits nervously at the table.

Why was this man asking me about my mother, about my birth date? She asks herself.

Suddenly she realizes why and thought about who he might be. Andrew finally looks at her. Lydia sits back in her seat. Andrew can't speak as he sees in her eyes what she has now realized. He slowly nods his head, answering the question that he could tell that she is asking but did not utter verbally. Tears form in her eyes—Andrew's heartbreaks. Lydia looks away and quickly wipes her tears away.

"Why am I just now meeting you?" she asks.

"Because I just now knowing of you." He answers.

"What?"

"Your mom and I, our marriage was complicated."

"Complicated?" Lydia asked. "Was there abuse?"

"No!" Andrew exclaimed, not realizing how loud he responds. "No," he said softly. "Lydia, I loved your mother. She didn't well..., she didn't want the same things."

Lydia shakes her head, not understanding; Andrew begins to explain.

"Our marriage, it was business. I needed a favor, and she needed a favor, so it was supposed to be temporary, two years. But within those two years, we fell in love-I fell in love,

I wanted her to stay but-,"

"Why didn't she stay?"

"I wish I knew Lydia; she was so guarded. There would be days when it seemed she was so happy, and then there were the days when she would withdraw."

"When did you find out about me?"

"I first saw you sing last week. You looked so familiar, but I couldn't put my finger on why at first. Then yesterday,

Another Slice of Pie

when you sang your mom's favorite song, I realized why you looked familiar. You look so much like your mother when she was young, and your music, your mother, wrote those songs."

Lydia nods. Andrew grins.

"Your name, Lydia Rose; I said that if I had a daughter, I would name her Lydia Rose."

Lydia looks away. It is quiet for a moment.

"I'm sorry, Lydia," Andrew says. "Your mom must have been pregnant when we got divorced. I swear if I had any idea-,"

"I asked her about my father; she just said that he's not around. I assumed he didn't want any children", Lydia said as tears fell from her eyes.

Andrew wants to reach out to her and hold her.

"No, no, I promised you," Andrew said in a soft tone, looking her directly in her eyes. "I would have never abandoned you if I had any idea that you existed."

"Mr. Gallagher, are you sure?" Lydia asks, taking her hands to whip her eyes. "Maybe you think you're my dad because of your time with my mom-,"

"No, I remember our time together, besides we can talk to her-,"

He stops talking when he sees Lydia shaking her head.

"Mom died two years ago," Lydia tells him. "She didn't want a big deal, so it was a small memorial."

Andrew waits for a moment. Robin is gone again. How did a successful musician manage to die without the world knowing? Knowing Robin's elusiveness, he shouldn't be surprised.

"How did she die?"

"Her asthma," Lydia answers.

Andrew shakes his head. He begins to mourn for her.

E. Davis
"She wouldn't take her medicine," they both said.

✦

Nathaniel and Naomi invited Robin and Andrew to the Gallagher cabin for the annual Gallagher family vacation.

"My mom, sister, and aunts cook. My nieces and nephews, cousins, play games, while my father and uncles smoke cigars, drink brandy, and talk politics and money."

"Sounds like the event of the season!" Robin joked.

"We don't have to go," Andrew said. "We can say that we have plans-,"

"No, let's go," she said with a grin.

"Yeah,"

"Yeah, sounds like fun," she said with a smile.

That particular summer weekend promised cloudless blue skies, plenty of sunshine, and high humidity. The usual atmosphere was beyond beautiful. The scenery promised serenity, but the humidly contradicted the full enjoyment. Robin never told anyone, but she had asthma. Although she somewhat grew out of the ailment, every once in the rarest blue moons. Robin limited herself to specific activities by avoiding specific settings where an attack would be invited, but the Gallagher family cabin was a setting and an activity that could not be avoided. The housekeepers managed to air out the home with the central air, but there was one bedroom that was seldom used, which happened to be Andrew's room. Considering that it had been some time since he attended these family outings, no one knew that the vent and register was broken. So the cool air did not circulate throughout the room properly. However, Andrew was more concerned about sleeping arrangements.

"If you're uncomfortable sharing a room-," Andrew begins.

Another Slice of Pie

"Don't be silly," she said, smiling. "Besides, what would your family think?"

Andrew grinned,

"I could sleep on the floor,"

Robin shook her head.

"Andrew, that won't be necessary, as long as I can have the left side," she told him with a smile.

He smiled back.

"Would you like a tour of the grounds?"

"Sure,"

While Andrew gave Robin a tour of the estate, Naomi noticed them. They seemed to be happy. There weren't any forced smiles or strained signs of affection. She noticed them holding hands how they would lean into each other when they shared a secret or laugh. Later on that evening, Andrew noticed that Robin seemed short-winded, as if she was trying to catch her breath. Andrew also noticed her wheezing.

"You feeling okay," Andrew asked, pulling her aside.

"Yes, my asthma, it's bothering me,"

"You need to phone in a prescription? There is a drug store a few miles-,"

"No, no, Andrew, I'm okay," she said with an assuring smile.

Later that night, Andrew was in the den writing in a journal, and Robin was in bed asleep. However, she found herself suddenly coughing and gasping for air. Robin got out of bed and tried to open the window, but with her coughing, she was too weak. She was using whatever energy she had for breathing. Soon she was feeling light-headed, she tried to pound on the window in hopes of breaking it, but she was so weak that the only thing she was doing was tapping the window. Meanwhile, in the den, Andrew decided that he wrote all that he needed to write. He began to head towards his room. On his way, he saw Nathaniel.

"Dad," Andrew said, acknowledging his father.

Nathaniel nodded his head with a grin.

"Were you writing?"

"Yes, sir."

"How are things?"

"Going well," Andrew replied.

Nathaniel smiled,

"Robin enjoying herself?"

"Yeah, she is," Andrew answered.

"You two seemed to be doing well," Nathaniel said.

Andrew grinned.

"Join me for a nightcap," Nathaniel suggested.

Nathaniel was reaching out. He saw that his son was no longer the goofy kid that he once was. Before Andrew could agree to his father's invitation, they heard a tapping sound.

"A mouse," Nathaniel asked.

"Mice, don't tap Dad," Andrew said.

Together, Nathaniel and Andrew followed the tapping. It led to Andrew's room. Andrew heard coughing. Suddenly Andrew remembered Robin's asthma. He quickly opened the door and was caught off guard by the humid air that came from the room.

"Robin!" he called out, "Dad, why is it so hot in here?"

Andrew quickly turned the light switch on. Nathaniel and Andrew found Robin on the floor. She wasn't tapping on the window, but she was tapping on the floor. She was sweating and gasping for air.

"Robin! Oh-," Andrew said, kneeling down.

He placed his hand on the vent.

Another Slice of Pie

"I was- try-ing, to open the wind-ow," she said, gasping for air.

Nathaniel checked the window and saw that it was locked, and the lock was broken, no air and no ventilation.

"What's going on?" Naomi asked, suddenly appearing.

"The window is broken; I never got around to having it fixed," Nathaniel admitted.

"Dad, this vent is broken too," Andrew said, checking the register.

Both men looked at Robin gasping for air sitting on the floor.

"I'm calling a doctor!" Nathaniel exclaimed.

"No doctors!" Robin stated breathlessly.

"Robin, where is your medicine," Andrew asked.

He lifted Robin up and picked her up in his arms.

"Just cool air, please," she pleaded.

Quickly many members of the family came from their sleeping quarters to see what was happening. Andrew led Robin to the living room. Someone had opened the door and windows to allow fresh air to circulate.

"Has someone called the doctor?" someone asked.

"No, doctors, Andrew, please," Robin pleaded.

"Robin-,"

"Please," she pleaded.

"Tell me what to do?" Andrew requested.

"Hot coffee," she said.

"Hot coffee," One asked.

She nodded and then pointed to the chair.

"Let me sit," Andrew sat her down on the chair.

He looked at her, wondering what to do next for her.

"It's hard for me to sit up, rub my back; it helps."

E. Davis

Immediately Andrew began to rub Robin's back. He wanted to cry; his heart was breaking. Why didn't check the room? He knew that it was stuffy, but he didn't make sure that it was clear. Andrew wanted to hug Robin and hold her in his arms, promising her that she would be okay. But he just continued to rub her back.

"Here, honey," said a member of the family, handing her a cup of coffee.

"Thank you," Robin said softly.

"What happened?" one asked.

"Dad forgot to have the window and the vent fixed, so the cool air from the central air didn't circulate," Andrew answered.

Nathaniel kneeled before Robin. The great Nathaniel was humbled.

"Honey, I am so sorry. I completely forgot. That room is hardly used."

"It's okay," Robin said as her chest whistled.

Nathaniel looked at Andrew, and he rubbed Robin's back.

"Honey, what didn't you tell us about your asthma?" Naomi asked.

"It was bothering her all day," Andrew mentioned.

"Robin!" Naomi admonished.

"I'll be okay," Robin said, still short of breath.

"Robin, please let us call a doc-,"

"No, I will be okay, I promise,"

"Move us to another room," Andrew said sternly.

"It's been done, Mr. Gallagher," one of the servants said.

After some time, everyone left Robin and Andrew alone. He was no longer rubbing her back but sitting on the

Another Slice of Pie

floor beside her. Robin had finished her coffee and her able to breathe with only a little struggle. Robin was tried. She managed to stand up, Andrew quickly stood up.

"What do you need?"

"I'm ready to go to bed," she said.

Andrew escorted Robin into their new room. The cool air was comforting—Robin collapse down on the bed.

"Robin," Andrew said.

She looked at him.

"Why didn't you say anything?"

As Robin sat up, Andrew sat next to her.

"I haven't had an attack in years. The medicine I used to be on, I would make me feel so weird and loopy."

"They make medicine now that-,"

"I know, I know, but I thought I outgrew it," Robin said.

"What does the coffee do?"

"An old wives tale says hot coffee stops an asthma attack." She answered.

Robin saw the concerned look in Andrew's eyes.

"Andrew, I'm okay,"

Andrew nodded his head, still not convinced. She wrapped her arms around him, catching him off guard. He welcomed the affection, Andrew hugged her back.

"Thank you for taking care of me," she said.

"You're welcome," he whispered.

Being in each other's arms felt nice; neither wanted the other to let go, but Robin eventually pulled away. They looked into each other's eyes and saw peace. To Andrew it was nice to see a vulnerable side to her; a side that appreciated the closeness that they were sharing at this moment. Andrew was sweet, tender, and sensitive. Robin never met a man or knew a man like him. He was someone that she could trust, and

E. Davis

based on this evening, Andrew was someone she could rely on. The way he took care of her showed his family he was a devoted husband. And it showed her that he was a good friend.

Looking at each other, Robin felt safe in his presence. Robin was tired and exhausted. She wanted to lay her head on his chest, get intoxicated by his cologne, close her eyes and sleep forever. Robin looked delicate, like a flower. Andrew saw that she wanted to rest upon him. He wanted to hold her.

"I want to sleep now," she said softly.

Andrew nodded her head.

Together they laid down on the bed, and without realizing it, they slept in each other's arms.

5

LYDIA LISTENS TO ANDREW tell her about her mother. Here is a man, proclaiming to be her father. Although the news is overwhelming, this stranger has honesty in his eyes, and there is a genuine nature to his demeanor. Why would her mother keep him from her or her from him?

"When did you know you loved her?" Lydia asks.

"I think, or I believed that night, it was tough to detect because I liked her. We were friends; we enjoyed each other's company."

Do you think she loved you back?" Lydia asked.

"She loved me," Andrew said. "I know she loved me."

"If you were such a great guy-"Lydia began, "Why would she leave?"

"I don't know, Lydia, I wish I knew," Andrew answered.

✦

They were married for over a year, and living together seemed natural. They went out to dinner together, went to the movies together. The world saw them together. It seemed as if they were the perfect couple. They were seen together smiling and relaxing, having fun. Their first time together, intimately, of course, was not planned. That particular Saturday evening, Andrew and Robin decided to stay home. There weren't any planned social events that Naomi insisted on their appearance, and there weren't any family functions that required their attendance. So that night, Andrew needed to write while Robin worked on some music. Considering their careers, their year went well. Robin began

E. Davis

writing music for Broadway plays, and movie producers have recognized her to write scores for upcoming movies. Andrew had a book published, and he currently was on the best sellers' list. For both Robin and Andrew, the writing was soothing. They were able to escape any kind of pressure from the outside and be free with their creativity.

However, Andrew was wrestling with writer's block. He balled up a piece of paper and tossed it behind him without realizing he had hit Robin on the head.

"You okay," Robin asked.

Andrew turned around and looked at Robin. She was holding the wad of paper in her hands. Andrew realized that he hit her.

"Robin, I am so sorry," he said, then laughed. "Writer's block,"

"Me too," she said. "Change in pace,"

She began to pick up the wads of paper from off the floor.

"How about we strike up the grill, eat ribs, and listen to some jazz."

"As long as you make those Daiquiris," Andrew said.

Barbeque, jazz, and alcohol are dangerous combinations for those who are trying to conceal their true feelings from one another. Both Robin and Andrew were somewhat buzzed from the amount of alcohol that they had drunk but sober enough to be clear in their actions. Together, Robin and Andrew sat on the balcony feeling stuffed from the food and cool from the breeze. The full moon made Robin seem almost angelic.

Robin attempted to clear the table, but Andrew stopped her, "Robin, let's dance," he took her by the hands.

"Let me clean up,"

Another Slice of Pie

"No, come on," Andrew said smiling.

Andrew took Robin by the hands and began to dance on the balcony. They had never danced together. At first, it seemed awkward.

"Did you enjoy din-," Robin began, but Andrew cut her off.

"Shh," he said softly.

He pulled her closed to him, and within moments they move instinctively. The smell of her perfume was intoxicating to him.

"You smell good," he said softly.

She didn't respond; she just danced with him. The rhythm of the music was hypnotizing her. His hazel eyes captivated her; they looked like beautiful stones of amber. Robin wrapped her arms around his shoulders, and without realizing the emotion they were caught up in, Andrew leaned in and began to kiss Robin. He caught himself, slowly pulled back, almost sorry for kissing her, but not sorry enough because he hoped that she wanted him to do it again. She looked up at him; her moon-shaped eyes said, "Kiss me again, please," He leaned in and kissed her again.

Suddenly the rain fell. Robin and Andrew quickly ran inside the apartment. Neither of them wanted this evening, their evening, to end, and so they picked up where they had left off. Andrew approached Robin; he cupped her face in his palms and began to kiss her again.

There were no convictions or feelings of remorse. Technically they were married. Andrew was not going to convince himself on why making love to his wife was wrong when emotionally being with Robin felt right. Again, it felt good to be at this place. In each other's arms holding each other. Here were two lonely people who didn't need to be lonely. As they lay in each other's arms, in the core of passion, neither of them wanted to the other to pull from their embrace. As their bodies lay intertwined, Andrew softly caressed Robin's back.

"Robin," he said softly

"Hmm,"

"This, this, feels nice," Andrew said.

Robin looked up at him. He smiled at her; her smile was faint. She kissed his chest then rested her head on him again.

Robin was not one for commitments. She had a no-strings-attached policy in life. Although there was a genuine affection for one another, she loved Andrew, but she wanted nothing more from this so-called relationship. She enjoyed being with Andrew in every phase of their relationship. She enjoyed spending Sunday afternoons with him just hanging around the apartment, playing the piano. Robin even enjoyed the organized events that she attended with him and his family. The quiet nights were they somehow managed to be up under a blanket watching a scary movie. She hid her eyes on his chest and the scary parts while he laughed. Robin considered Andrew a friend, a good friend, at this stage in life, practically her best friend. There was a sense of security with this relationship and that there was no promised commitment, the security of no broken hearts.

Andrew wanted more to make this hoax of a marriage real. He loved Robin, but he wasn't going to press this issue, but he enjoyed the time he had with her, and he did his best to focus on his writing. However, when the two-year mark came, Andrew was more in love than he should have been. One night they lay in bed, naked under the covers.

"Robin, stay with me," he said as he whispered.

Another Slice of Pie

He softly kissed her back. Robin turned over to face him. She smiled at him, but her heart and mind were fixed.

That day, the day she left, he pleaded with her, almost begging her not to go.

"Robin," he said, cupping her face in his palms.

Tears fell from her eyes.

"I know you love me," he said.

"I can't stay," she said, pulling back, "Don't make this hard-,"

"Robin," he said now crying, "Baby, we are already married-,"

"No," Robin said. "No, I need my music, my freedom."

"Freedom, what freedom," he asked confused. "I know that you love me, you wouldn't make love to me the way that you do if you didn't love me-,"

"Don't-," Robin says, smiling.

"You wouldn't do the little things you do for me if you didn't love-,"

"Andrew, please-,"

"Robin, look me in the eyes and tell me that you don't love me,"

She wiped the tears from her eyes and looked him directly in the eyes,

"Don't make this harder than it needs to be." She said. "This was business,"

"It was, but baby; this now can be love,"

Stunned but not shocked was the world's reaction to the divorce of Andrew and Robin. The couple that showed so much promise had called it quits.

What happened? What went wrong? Who was the one that filed? Were the questions that went forth from the social scene.

E. Davis

Nathaniel had his suspicions at first, but throughout the two years, the Gallagher family grew to love Robin. She was sweet, intelligent, and most importantly, she did not bring shame to the family.

Nathaniel and Andrew sat on the balcony one evening, the same balcony that Robin and he danced on, both of them drinking brandy. Although the air was hot and humid, Andrew wore an old pair of gray sweatpants and a t-shirt while Nathaniel wore a three-piece suit.

"I loved her," Andrew said. "I truly loved her."

"Was there someone else?" Nathaniel asked.

Herself, Andrew wanted to say, but instead, he answered;

"No,"

"You'll be okay, son," Nathaniel said, consoling his son.

Andrew didn't respond. Instead, he just looked at the sunset.

Andrew kept his promise not to let Robin be bad-mouthed. She was not to be called a gold digger. When the marriage was over, she left with the money that she accumulated from her music. There was never a strong desire to remarry. Andrew just focused on his career.

✦

"TELL ME ABOUT YOU, about your life," Andrew said.

"What do you want to know?" Lydia asks.

"Where did you grow up?" he asks.

"Boston," she answers. "I came to Manhattan a month ago,"

"When did you start singing?"

"All my life," Lydia answered. "Mom would play the piano, and I would sing the notes of the keys."

Another Slice of Pie

Andrew grins.

"What happens now?" Lydia asks.

"Whatever you want," Andrew said. "I would like to be a part of your life, but it is up to you,"

Lydia takes a deep breath. She sips her tea. Still, she is trying to take this sudden information in. Every aspect of her mother's personality and mannerisms were true. Robin was distant when it came down to certain matters and situations. However, Lydia knew of another Robin, Robin Booker, the mother. The mother would make sure that she would kiss Lydia Rose every night each night and greet her with open arms every morning to welcome in her day.

Robin had a busy schedule, writing music for successful singers. Her music won them Grammys. She also won Tony awards, and she had written musical scores for Oscar-winning movies. But, no matter how successful Robin was, Lydia was a priority. They had weekend slumber parties, shopping, eating out, painted each other's toenails.

"She never had any boyfriends, none that I knew of. There were many admirers, though. My mom was really beautiful."

Andrew nods her head.

"I heard of her success, but you-,"

"She was very adamant about her personal life. Mom was very private. I understand why. You know, once the media gets wind of me being your daughter; you and my mother's daughter, it will get crazy."

"I don't care," Andrew said. "Your mother and I hid what was real for too long. It's time to stop hiding."

"Coming out with an illegitimate daughter, with your background and how private my mother was?"

E. Davis

"You're not illegitimate," Andrew said. "You were conceived in love and marriage. I promised your mother that she would not be bad mouthed. I can stand by her decision on

keeping you out of the public eye. So this will be that we kept you out of the public eye until we were ready; hence now, your career."

Lydia nods her head with a smile.
"What do I call you?" she asks.
"Whatever you're comfortable with," Andrew says.
Lydia finishes the last piece of her pie.
"Would you like another slice of pie?" Andrew asks.
Lydia grins,
"Sure,"

Made in the USA
Middletown, DE
27 July 2024